Kai's Kite:
I Belive I Can, So I Will

About the Author:
Dr. Shana J. is a passionate storyteller, educator, and dreamer who believes in the power of words to inspire and transform. As the founder of Ed.Dukated Expressions, LLC, she creates books and resources that encourage children and adults alike to believe in themselves, embrace new possibilities, and never stop learning.
Her work often reflects her love for family, faith, and the lessons life teaches through perseverance and courage. Kai's Kite was inspired by her nephew, Kai, and the joy of welcoming new life into the world. For Dr. Shana, this book is more than a story—it's a celebration of hope and belief.
When she isn't writing, Dr. Shana loves to travel, explore new cultures, and spend time with her loved ones. She hopes every reader who turns the pages of her books feels uplifted, encouraged, and ready to soar.

For Kai,
From the very moment I learned you were on the way,
this story began to take shape in my heart.
You are the inspiration for these pages—
the reminder that belief, determination, and love can lift
us higher than the strongest wind.
May you always know that you were prayed for,
 dreamed of, and deeply loved—long before you
took your very first breath.
With all my love,
Dr. J

On a bright, breezy morning,
Kai woke up with excitement buzzing through him.

Today was the day he would finally
get to fly his shiny new kite!

He had **worked so hard**
putting it together all

by himself, and now,
it was **ready to soar.**

With a big smile,
Kai ran outside.

The wind was perfect,
just strong enough to
lift his kite into the sky.

He held the string tightly,
took a deep breath,
and let the kite go.

But instead of soaring, it wobbled,
spun in circles, and crashed down
to the grass with a soft thud.
"**Oh no,**" Kai sighed, staring at his fallen kite.

oooOHHhh NOoooo!

Why won't it fly?
It's never going to work!

"Feeling discouraged, Kai trudged
back inside to find his dad."

"Dad," he said, his voice
    a little sad, "I tried so hard,

but my kite won't fly.
    I don't think I can do it."

His dad looked up from his work and smiled. "Well, sometimes things don't work the first time, Kai," he said. But you know what? The trick to flying a kite **—like anything else—is to keep trying.**

You don't have to get it perfect right away. You just have to **believe you can do it, and try again.**

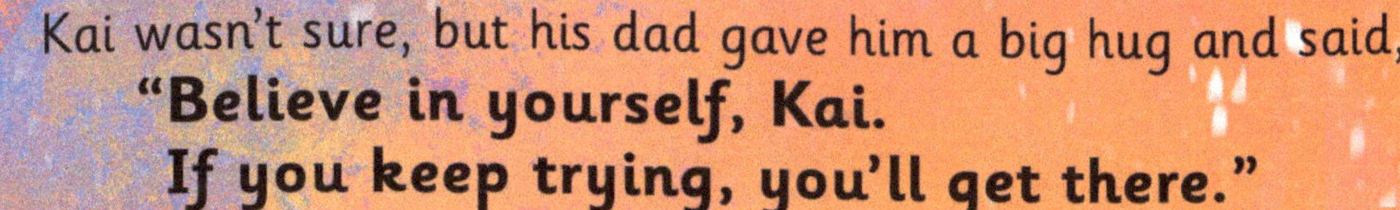

Kai wasn't sure, but his dad gave him a big hug and said,
**"Believe in yourself, Kai.
If you keep trying, you'll get there."**

Kai looked down at his kite, feeling a little better.
"Okay, Dad. I believe I can, so I will!"
His dad smiled. **"That's the spirit!"**

With new determination, Kai grabbed his kite and decided to make it even more special. "I want to decorate it!" he said. **He added little pictures of soccer balls, race cars, and stars. Now the kite was as unique as him!**

Back outside, Kai and his dad **worked together to make sure the string was just right.**

The wind was perfect, and Kai was ready. **He stood tall, held the kite up,** and slowly let the string out.

The kite wobbled at first, but then...
it started to climb!
Higher and higher,
the kite danced with the wind.

His dad grinned.
"I knew you could do it, Kai!
You just had to believe you could."

"Dad, look! It's flying!"
Kai shouted, jumping up and down.

The kite soared above,
twisting and turning in the sky.

Kai was filled with joy, and his dad was proud.
"See?" his dad said. **"When you believe in yourself, there's nothing you can't do."**

Kai's heart felt full as he looked up at the sky.
He had made his kite fly. And it felt amazing!
"Dad," Kai said, grinning,
"I believe I can, so I will!"
That's the motto! his dad agreed with a smile.
"Remember, it's not just about kites."

You can do anything if you believe in yourself.
As Kai's kite flew high, he realized that
believing in yourself made all the difference
—not just in flying kites,
but in everything.

With a big smile, Kai thought,
I can climb mountains, I can solve problems,
I can try new things —because if
I believe I can, I will!

And as the sun shone bright,
Kai's kite soared on the wind,
just like his dreams.

www.ingramcontent.com/pod-product-compliance
Lightning Source LLC
Chambersburg PA
CBHW041203100726
47911CB00016B/841